Disney

FROZEN II

SPIRITS OF THE Enchanted Forest

Adapted by Marilyn Easton

studio fun
INTERNATIONAL

One night in the kingdom of Arendelle, a strong wind blew down the empty streets. So strong that it pushed Arendellians out of their homes toward the nearby cliffs. The shocked villagers turned to their queen, Elsa, for guidance.

Then Grand Pabbie and the trolls arrived! "You woke the spirits of nature. Whatever possessed you, child?" Grand Pabbie asked Elsa.

Elsa explained that a mysterious voice was calling to her from the north, from inside the Enchanted Forest. She planned to go to the Enchanted Forest, find the voice, and, hopefully, discover some answers.

"You must be careful. The spirits are still very angry and very powerful. They will challenge you every step of the way," Grand Pabbie warned.

With that, Elsa, Anna, Kristoff, Sven, and Olaf began their journey into the unknown.

When they arrived at the forest, the group saw a sparkling mist. It wouldn't let anyone in—or out. Anna and Elsa stood before the mist hand in hand—then the mist pulled back and allowed them to enter.

Before them stood four tall monoliths, each with a unique symbol that represented a different spirit of nature. As they continued to explore the Enchanted Forest, the group saw the dam that protected Arendelle from flooding. It had been built by Elsa and Anna's grandfather, King Runeard, as a gift of peace to a nomadic people called the Northuldra.

Suddenly, Olaf was swept up in a powerful windstorm. Olaf's friends rushed to help him, but the Wind Spirit swept them up, too. Elsa flooded the vortex with snow magic. There was a flash of white, and the tornado stopped.

The air cleared and left behind ice sculptures that depicted memories of the past. Anna noticed someone familiar in one showing a young man being saved by a Northuldra girl.

"Father? That's father," said Anna.

Then a whirling sound came from the trees, and the bushes shook. A group of Arendellian soldiers and Northuldra appeared. They had been stuck inside the Enchanted Forest for several years.

"Listen, someone or something called me here," Elsa explained to the curious strangers. "If I can just find them, I know they have the answers we need to free this forest."

Suddenly, the Fire Spirit appeared! It set trees ablaze and left a burning trail in its path. Elsa tried her best to put out the flames, but she struggled to keep up.

The chaos paused. Elsa noticed the Fire Spirit was actually a tiny salamander. Elsa held out her hand for it to climb into. The Fire Spirit calmed down, and the flames extinguished. Then Elsa heard the voice again.

Anna was relieved that no one was harmed, but she was upset that Elsa took such a risk fighting the fire. To comfort her, Elsa wrapped their mother's scarf around Anna's shoulders. The Northuldra gasped and whispered.

"That's a *Northuldra* scarf," said Ryder.

"What?" Anna replied with confusion. "It was our mother's."

Elsa led everyone to the ice sculpture of their father as a young man. They recognized that the Northuldra girl saving their father was their mother. The Northuldra embraced Elsa and Anna, welcoming them into their community.

That night, Honeymaren revealed something else. The diamond symbol on their mother's scarf represented a fifth spirit of nature: the bridge between humans and the magic of nature, according to legend.

Then the ground shook—Earth Giants were passing through the camp. Everyone hid. Eventually, the giants left, unable to locate what they were searching for.

"The giants sensed me. I don't want them coming back here and putting everyone at risk again. We're going now," said Elsa. Anna and Olaf followed her, but Kristoff and Sven were nowhere to be found.

As they traveled north, the Wind Spirit returned, sweeping around Elsa. It led her eyes to a tattered flag in the distance. The sisters and Olaf headed in that direction. They were not prepared for what they discovered.

It was a shipwreck lying in a dry riverbed—the ship belonged to Elsa and Anna's parents. The heartbroken sisters searched for clues and uncovered a map to Ahtohallan—a magical river said to hold the answers about the past.

"Honeymaren said there was a fifth spirit, a bridge between the magic of nature and us," Elsa said. "That's who's been calling me . . . from Ahtohallan. The answers about the past are all there."

"So we go to Ahtohallan," said Anna.

"Not WE . . . *me*," Elsa replied. "The Dark Sea is too dangerous for us both to cross."

With that, Elsa created a boat and sent Anna and Olaf gliding down a path made of ice. Elsa told them she would send a signal when she reached her destination—then she was on her own.

When she arrived at the Dark Sea, Elsa saw a
landmass in the distance. But wave after ferocious wave
roared between her and her destination. With bravery
and determination, she was ready for whatever came next.

Elsa took a deep breath before diving into the turbulent sea where she faced the Water Nokk. After several different challenges, Elsa created an ice bridle that she tossed onto the back of the wild spirit. She rode the Water Nokk to the other side of the Dark Sea.

When Elsa reached the shore, she saw a glacier. Of course, Ahtohallan was a frozen river! Memories of the past played before her. A vision of her grandfather appeared, revealing his true intention for building the dam. It wasn't a gift of peace for the Northuldra—it was a trick! King Runeard wanted to control the water and reshape the forest.

At that moment, Elsa felt something was very wrong. She had gone too far inside the glacier. Elsa sent a signal to Anna before Elsa was encased in the ice.

Meanwhile, Anna and Olaf floated past the sleeping Earth Giants into the Lost Caverns. They searched for an exit and came upon a fork in the path. That's when a strong blast came from the left tunnel—it was Elsa's signal!

Her signal formed a sculpture. It showed that King Runeard started the battle against the Northuldra.

"I know how to free the forest," said Anna. "We have to break the dam."

"But Arendelle will be flooded," Olaf replied.

"That's why everyone was forced out. To protect them from what must be done," Anna explained.

Anna was determined to right the past wrongs and save their kingdom; but first, she had to find a way out of the caverns. Then she needed to reunite with her sister so they could return to Arendelle—together.